Hanuman's Journey
to the
Medicine Mountain

Vatsala Sperling
Illustrated by Sandeep Johari

Bear Cub Books
Rochester, Vermont

❦

For Dada, Harish Johari

Bear Cub Books
One Park Street
Rochester, Vermont 05767
www.InnerTraditions.com

Bear Cub Books is a division of Inner Traditions International

Text copyright © 2006 by Vatsala Sperling
Artwork copyright © 2006 by Sandeep Johari

Library of Congress Cataloging-in-Publication Data

Sperling, Vatsala, 1961–
  Hanuman's journey to the medicine mountain / Vatsala Sperling ; illustrated by Sandeep Johari.
    p. cm.
  ISBN-13: 978-1-59143-063-6 (hardcover)
  ISBN-10: 1-59143-063-1 (hardcover)
  1. Hanumān (Hindu deity)—Juvenile literature. I. Johari, Sandeep, ill. II. Title.
  BL1225.H3S74 2006
  294.5'922045—dc22

                                                    2006015750

Printed and bound in India by Replika Press Pvt. Ltd.

10 9 8 7 6 5 4 3 2 1

Text design and layout by Priscilla Baker
This book was typeset in Berkeley, with Nueva and Abbess used as display typefaces

To send correspondence to the author of this book, mail a first-class letter to the author c/o Inner Traditions • Bear & Company, One Park Street, Rochester, VT 05767, and we will forward the communication.

Cast of Characters

Hanuman
(Han-oo-'mahn)
Son of the wind god
and minister of Sugriva,
servant of Ram

Sugriva
(Soo-'gree-va)
Deposed King of
the Monkeys

Ram
(Rahm)
Incarnation of Lord Vishnu on
Earth, Prince of Ayodhya

Lakshman
('Lahk-sh-mahn)
Brother of Ram, Prince
of Ayodhya

Sita
('See-tah)
Incarnation of Goddess
Lakshmi, wife of Ram

Sampati
('Sam-pa-tee)
King of the Vultures,
brother of Jatayu

Jambavan
(Jahm-ba-'vahn)
King of the Bears,
son of Lord Brahma

Indra
('In-dra)
King of the Lesser Gods,
ruler of rain and storms

Surasa
('Soor-a-sa)
A demon guarding
the ocean

Ravana
('Rah-va-'nah)
The ten-headed King
of the Demons

Vibhishana
(Vib-'heesh-a-na)
Ravana's younger brother,
Prince of Lanka

Indrajeet
('In-dra-jeet)
Son of Ravana

Brahma
(Brahm-'ha)
God of Creation

Vishnu
('Vish-noo)
God of Preservation

Shiva
(Shee-'va)
God of Creative Destruction

About Hanuman, the Magical Monkey

The Hindu people believe that long, long ago the ancient land of India was the playing field of gods and demons, sages and kings, and animals and birds, who performed miraculous feats in a never ending contest between the forces of good and the forces of evil.

One story about the victory of good over evil is a famous epic poem from India called the Ramayana, which was written in the Sanskrit language by the Hindu sage Valmiki. Ram, the hero of this epic, is believed to be Lord Vishnu, God of Preservation, born on Earth in human form. Ram wages war against Ravana, the evil demon king. In his battle against Ravana, Ram receives help from many animals, the most notable being Hanuman, a monkey with magical powers.

Born to Pavan, God of the Wind, and Anjana, a celestial nymph, Hanuman has many amazing abilities. Because he is devoted to Ram, Hanuman uses his magical skills to help Ram win the war. His story is a tale of courage, wisdom, and cleverness that inspires people to this day.

In modern India, monkeys are considered to be sacred beings. Hindus believe that whenever the Ramayana is recited, Hanuman will come to hear Ram's name spoken aloud. They pray to Hanuman when they feel weak or fearful, believing that he will arrive in his invisible form to help them solve their problems, just as once he helped Ram.

It was a bright afternoon on Rishyamook Mountain and the warm sun shimmered through the leaves of the jungle canopy. Sugriva, the exiled king of monkeys, and his minister, Hanuman, were doing just what monkeys love to do—basking in the treetops, lazily grooming each other. Suddenly they were interrupted by a distant cry, the sound of a woman's voice, desperately calling, "Help, oh please help me! Ram, help me! Ram!" It seemed as if the voice was coming from the heavens, and indeed, when they looked up, they saw a flash of light, like a streaking meteor. It was a chariot, racing across the clear blue sky. As they watched, a slender arm tossed a small bundle over the side. And then, rustling in the branches, a pouch came hurtling down through the thick canopy of the forest. Hanuman, who was one of the quickest beings on Earth or in heaven, caught it just before it hit the ground.

When the two monkeys opened the pouch, a handful of beautiful jewelry tumbled out onto the grass. "These must belong to the woman who was screaming for help," said Sugriva. They looked up at the sky again. The chariot was a mere speck, disappearing into thick clouds on the far horizon. The two monkeys looked at each other and their bright mood changed to sadness as they considered the poor woman's plight.

A few days later, a monkey scout reported to King Sugriva that he had seen two young armed men wandering near a lake. "They must be Vali's men," said Sugriva with an angry flick of his long tail. "My evil brother must have sent them to spy on me. Is he not satisfied with stealing my wife and banishing me from my own kingdom?" He clenched his fists.

But Hanuman was calmer. "We shouldn't jump to conclusions, O King," said Hanuman. "I will ask them who they are."

Hanuman, as you will see, had many amazing powers. He could change his form to whatever he liked, and he could even make himself invisible. So no one saw him as he soared above the treetops. When he reached the two men, he appeared before them as a young mendicant. Though the men were dressed in simple ochre robes, they glowed with an inner strength. Hanuman knew at once they could not be Vali's spies.

"Good sirs, with your grace and strength you look as though you could rule the world. Why do you wander in these deep and difficult woods? Please tell me who you are," said Hanuman politely.

"I am Ram. This is my younger brother, Lakshman. King Dasharatha, the late ruler of Ayodhya, was our father. My beloved wife, Sita, is missing. We are looking everywhere for her." As Ram spoke, he stared intently at the gold earring that Hanuman wore. Hanuman had worn this earring since birth, but no one had ever seen it—until now. When he was a little baby, Lord Brahma had said to him, "This earring will be invisible to all except Lord Vishnu. Born on Earth as Ram, only he will be able to see it. That is how you will recognize each other. All the magical powers I've given you will help you serve Ram."

Hanuman recalled those words and smiled. "Lord Ram, I am Hanuman." He took on his original appearance, that of a monkey, and spoke again, his eyes brimming with joy, "Climb onto my shoulders, and I will take you both to Sugriva."

On the way, Hanuman explained why King Sugriva was living in exile, and how the king's older brother, Vali, had stolen the kingdom, and had captured Sugriva's wife, Ruma. When they arrived at the top of Rishyamook Mountain, Hanuman gently lowered his passengers to the ground.

"King Sugriva, I have brought Ram and his brother Lakshman. Ram's wife, Sita, is missing, and they are searching for her," he said.

"Welcome," said Sugriva. "You are my guests and friends. We have something that might help you." Sugriva asked Hanuman to bring the jewelry pouch. When Ram opened it, he bowed his head, and then held the pouch to his lips. For a moment he seemed unable to speak. Then he cried, "Sita, my beloved Sita, where are you?"

"Grieve no more, my friend," said Sugriva. "Your Sita threw this from a chariot we saw flying south. I will have the entire Earth searched for her. We will find her safe, I swear."

Ram looked up. "And in return I will help you win back your kingdom and your wife, Ruma. I know all about Vali," he said. "He shall rule no more."

Ram kept his promise right away by slaying the arrogant Vali. Sugriva and Ruma were reunited, and Lakshman held a coronation ceremony for Sugriva. The whole monkey kingdom rejoiced to have their true king back. Sugriva was very happy—so happy, in fact, that he forgot all about his promise to Ram.

Ram was patient with the lengthy celebrations, for he understood how Sugriva had suffered. But he missed Sita, and grew anxious. The summer and then the rainy season came and went, and a chill settled over the land. Finally, Ram could wait no longer. Early one morning he asked Lakshman to remind Sugriva of his promise. Lakshman, who had also grown impatient with the passing months, was more than glad to help. "I'll go right now, my Lord," he said.

With a few long strides a furious Lakshman arrived at the door of King Sugriva's palace. Hanuman saw him approach, and ran to alert the monkey king.

"Sugriva, it is time to get up! Quick!" Hanuman shook the sleepy king's shoulder. "Wake up! Get to your feet and keep your promise. Help Ram as he helped you," he said.

Sugriva blinked and rubbed his eyes. *Hanuman is right, as always!* he thought. He ran out the door and bumped right into Lakshman, who stood on the doorstep seething with anger. Glaring at Sugriva, he bellowed, "How dare you forget your promise to my brother?"

"Forgive me, please. I will organize a search right away," Sugriva pleaded. "Please forgive me."

"Now. Do it now," hissed Lakshman. "You must not disappoint my brother Ram."

Very relieved to be forgiven, Sugriva called for his generals and sent them off in all directions, each with a huge contingent of animal soldiers. "Look for Sita everywhere you think she could be. Look for her everywhere you think she could *never* be. Report to me in a month," he said. Then he turned to Hanuman. "You have become very close to Ram. You should ask him for your marching orders."

Ram told Hanuman to follow the path of the flying chariot. "It was headed south. You, too, should travel south to find Sita. Give her this when you see her," Ram said, and handed his gold signet ring to Hanuman. When he held the ring up, Hanuman saw the name *Ram* inscribed on it, over and over: *Ram, Ram, Ram.*

"Serving you is my honor, Lord Ram," he said with humility.

King Sugriva asked Jambavan, King of the Bears, to guide the thousands of monkey soldiers who would accompany Hanuman. Jambavan was a very wise old bear. He was the son of Lord Brahma himself and knew the answers to many of life's puzzles and deepest questions.

Marching south, the monkeys looked in all the valleys and groves, lakes and streams, cottages, townships, and kingdoms. They left no stone unturned. They asked everyone they met for information. But they found no sign of the lost Sita. And finally, they could travel no farther south. Before them was the ocean—deep, mysterious, majestic, and endless.

Their spirits fell. Monkeys, after all, do not know how to swim. "We cannot return to Lord Ram empty handed," they said. They sat in rows on the hot, shimmering sand, their pained faces bowed low. Despairing, the animals decided to fast until death.

"Did I hear you speak the name 'Ram?'" A sad old vulture appeared. Unkempt and at death's door, he interrupted the monkeys' fast with a weak croak. "I am Sampati, King of the Vultures. Jatayu, my younger brother, was killed by Ravana, King of the Demons. Jatayu tried to stop Ravana's chariot and rescue Ram's wife. He fought bravely. He tried his best, but Ravana cut his wings." Sampati's breath was ragged with grief.

"Ravana is holding Sita captive on the island of Lanka, 800 miles south of here." The poor old vulture's voice began to fade. "Now that I have told you all I know of Sita, I can die in peace." Sampati's head fell, his eyes dimmed, and his spirit soared toward heaven.

The monkeys were happy to hear that Sita was alive, but they still had no idea how to reach her. "Maybe we can just jump to the island," suggested some of the younger, less experienced monkeys, but no one took them seriously. Monkeys can leap from branch to branch with ease, true, but they can't leap across an ocean.

Jambavan, however, knew better. "Hanuman, you never brag but I know you can cross the ocean. Let me remind you again of your birth—and all the magical boons that were bestowed upon you by Lord Brahma. Then you'll remember how you can do the impossible."

A murmur spread throughout the army. "There is hope, there is hope." Soon the murmur rose to a clamor.

"Tell us, Jambavan, tell us how Hanuman can save the day!"

Jambavan cleared his throat with a low growl and began to tell Hanuman's story.

❧

A celestial nymph was born on earth as Anjana, the daughter of a monkey king. When she grew up she married Kesari, the chief of another band of monkeys. She was very devoted and loyal to him. One day she took on a human form and went strolling on Rishyamook Mountain. The wind god Pavan was passing by and he saw her. She is perfect in every way, he thought. As Pavan moved toward her, Anjana felt the wind pick up, embracing her slender body, tossing her long dark hair, tugging at her silken robes. "Who dares touch me?" she asked, "I am married to Kesari. I am devoted to him."

"Anjana, it is I, God of the Wind," Pavan whispered softly. "Lord Brahma asked me to tell you that soon you will bear my son. He will be very wise and loyal to Lord Vishnu. He will be able to leap farther than the eye can see. He will be able to move even faster than I can."

"But why? Why must I bear your son?" Anjana asked.

"Lord Vishnu will need him on Earth, Anjana." Pavan whispered very softly, as quiet as thought itself.

That very evening Anjana gave birth to a little baby. He had a sweet rosy face, innocent golden eyes, and fine, sharp teeth. A sleek coat of silvery soft hair covered his agile little body. "What a perfect monkey you are, my son!" Anjana said lovingly. "Perfect in every way. Be success-ful in all that you are meant to do. Your father, Pavan, will be here soon to watch over you." Anjana kissed her newborn baby good-bye, and left him warm and safe at the entrance to a cave.

Baby Hanuman lay on his back, kicking his tiny feet and sucking his tiny fingers. As the night wore on, he started to feel hungry. At dawn, he noticed the rising sun.

Yum! A little plum! he thought, and took a leap. In that one leap he crossed the entire sky. *Higher and higher he flew.*

When Indra, the king of the lesser gods, saw the little monkey open his mouth to swallow up the sun, he was horrified. "No, no, no, my child! Don't touch! Hot! Hot! Don't eat that!" he shrieked, quickly hurling a thunderbolt at the unsuspecting baby. Hanuman came tumbling down onto Rishyamook Mountain and fell right in front of the cave where Pavan was waiting for him.

Furious to see his baby treated in such a rough manner, Pavan cradled Hanuman in his arms and retreated deep into the cave—taking the wind with him. The world grew completely still. Leaves ceased their dance in the breeze, birds soaring high above on currents of air plunged to earth. All of creation held its breath.

Lord Brahma quickly approached Pavan. "You must forgive Indra. He didn't mean to harm your son. He was only trying to keep the earth from freezing to death without the sun. Come back, Pavan," he pleaded. "You are the breath of life. Both Indra and I will give your son special boons. Your little baby will never know defeat, and he will grow to be very wise, loyal, and strong. He will take after you, Pavan. He will be invisible whenever he needs to be."

Pavan was pleased, and with a strong Whoosh! he blew back into the world. The whole world took a deep breath. The trees shook their leaves with relief, and once again the birds took to the skies. Pavan agreed to let Lord Shiva and his pet bull Nandi take charge of raising the baby Hanuman and educating him.

❧

Jambavan had reached the end of his story. "This is the story of your birth and all the boons that you have received, Hanuman. Sometimes, in your humility you might not remember how amazing you are. If there is one being here who can do the impossible, it is you. Now, go find Sita."

"Victory to Hanuman! Victory to Hanuman!" chanted all the monkeys, as Hanuman joyfully fluffed up his fur, swished his tail and took off over the open water with one enormous bound. They watched until he disappeared from view.

Nothing could stand in Hanuman's way. When he was gobbled up by the demon Surasa on the way to Lanka, he escaped with ease. He simply made himself as small as a fly and traveled up to Surasa's nostrils, tickling the inside of her nose. *Aachoo!* Surasa sneezed a mighty sneeze, and out flew Hanuman. He buzzed off and continued on his way before she could raise a hand to swat him.

Hanuman landed on the northern shore of Lanka just as the sun was setting. Under cover of night, he crept up to King Ravana's palace. He saw demons of all types—large and small, bony and fat. Some looked scary, some looked ferocious, some looked sneaky, and some looked mean but none of them looked sleepy. They were creatures of the night, at home in the dark.

But somewhere one of them was asleep. Of this Hanuman was sure, for he heard the faint but persistent echo of a rumbling snore. When he followed the sound to its source, he found himself facing a magnificent door, inlaid with pearls and gemstones. He opened the door gently and saw a huge golden bed, studded with thousands of diamonds. On it lay Ravana, the monstrous demon king himself. His ten awful heads rested on ten silken pillows.

Well, I've found Ravana, thought Hanuman. *But I know Sita is not here—*
she would never, never stay near such a creature. I will look for her at daylight.

The
next day,
Hanuman
swung through the
treetops, scanning the entire
city for a sign of the lovely Sita. Finally he stopped in
the Ashoka grove. He sat hidden among the branches of a
Sansapa tree and prayed to the gods for help. As he prayed, he
heard a commotion—heavy footsteps, loud snorts, and grunts
grew closer and closer, louder and louder. Cautiously, he parted
the thick leaves and peered out.

A huge dark form loomed menacingly, slowly approaching the very tree
in which Hanuman was hiding. Many demons marched alongside the giant
figure. One fanned him. Another sprinkled rose petals in his path, while
another held an umbrella over his ten heads. The entire
procession stopped right below Hanuman. He
could almost have reached out and snatched
Ravana's umbrella.

And then he looked down and saw the beautiful woman who sat beneath the tree. Sita! He had found her at last! He could barely keep himself from whooping with joy. But he quietly bided his time.

"I order you to love me, Sita," said the arrogant Ravana. "Your worthless husband can't even find me, much less defeat me in battle. Forget him. Be mine." All ten heads spoke at once, and all twenty eyes glittered with desire.

Needless to say, Sita was not the least bit charmed—nor was she afraid. "You are a fool to think I would ever love you," she said. "You came in a cowardly disguise and lured my husband away in order to steal me. You did not dare to fight Ram openly, in honest battle. Know this: I will never be yours." She spoke with indignation and contempt in her clear, soft voice.

"Beware, Sita. Do not try my patience. I will return tomorrow," Ravana said. He stomped away angrily, his entourage trailing behind him.

Sita waited until he was truly gone, and then allowed herself to fall to the ground and weep. "I would rather die than be Ravana's wife! How I miss Ram! Why am I still alive?"

"So that you will be with Ram again," Hanuman whispered to her, speaking in a secret animal language in case any demons were still lurking and listening.

Sita sat up. She looked around, wiping the tears from her eyes. "Who speaks?" she asked in the same secret language.

"I am Hanuman. Lord Ram has sent me to look for you."

"How did you get here?

"I jumped over the ocean."

"Why should I believe that? How can I be sure you are not one of Ravana's spies?"

"Will this ring prove to you that I am indeed Lord Ram's messenger?" asked Hanuman. He jumped down and showed Ram's signet ring to Sita. Sita took the ring with trembling fingers. She bowed her head and kissed it, saying softly, "Ram, my dearest, where are you? Ram, come soon and set me free." Then she gave Hanuman her barrette to take to Ram. "Thank you," she said. "What a courageous monkey you are! May your trip back be safe and swift."

But before Hanuman journeyed back, he wanted to see Ravana face-to-face. Standing there in the grove, he made himself taller than the oldest, grandest tree. Then he plucked the tree, just as if it were a rather large turnip, and swung it at a group of demon spies. He picked up huge boulders as if they were mere pebbles and hurled them too.

One of the spies ran to tell Ravana, "I saw a monkey, O King. Just a monkey. But what a powerful monkey he was! He threw a tree at my head! A HUGE tree!"

"Bring that monkey to my court! Now!" ordered Ravana.

When Hanuman saw the band of demon soldiers approaching, he shrank back to his normal size. *This is my chance to meet the demon king,* he thought to himself with satisfaction.

"Now that you have had your fun, monkey, it is our turn," the soldiers said, and they dragged Hanuman to the palace. Hanuman let them hit him and kick him. But they had no idea how powerful he really was.

"Monkey, who are you? Why are you here?" Ravana asked.

"I am Hanuman. I am here because Lord Ram sent me," said Hanuman. "Sita will never love you. Set her free, O King, and Lord Ram will forgive you." As Hanuman spoke, his tail began to grow and coil beneath him. The coil grew as tall as Ravana's mighty throne, and Hanuman, sitting atop that coil, faced Ravana eyeball-to-eyeball.

Ravana did not like hearing the bitter truth about Sita. His twenty eyes glared with rage and would not meet Hanuman's gaze.

"Kill this monkey now!" he thundered.

The demons hastened to do his bidding, but Vibhishana, Ravana's younger brother, stepped forward to stop them. "You cannot kill a messenger. You know that, Ravana. It is the law. You can injure him if you really find it necessary, but you cannot kill him."

"Burn his tail, then. That will teach him a lesson. Monkeys love their tails," ordered Ravana, glaring irritably at his brother. *Vibhishana is so meddlesome! I'll have to get rid of him soon,* he thought. He had never liked his just and truthful younger brother. Vibhishana was a great devotee of Lord Vishnu and often disagreed with Ravana's cruel policies.

The guards brought oil-soaked rags and began to wrap them around Hanuman's tail. But the tail kept growing—no matter how fast they worked, they always had more tail to wrap.

After they
used up all the
rags and oil from
the palace, they borrowed
more from the houses nearby. The tired guards wiped their sweaty brows
and stretched their stiff limbs and wrapped and wrapped and wrapped.
Finally, when the tail was more or less covered, they lit the very tip.

Hah! Right before their eyes, Hanuman's tail shrank back to its normal
size and he bounced out the window. Soon he was hopping over the
rooftops and the trees of the city. Using the tip of his tail like a torch, he
started fires with every leap, until the entire city of Lanka was ablaze.
Then he delicately dipped the tip of his tail in the ocean, and with a
sizzle, the flame went out.

Back in the Ashoka grove, the gentle Sita saw the flames leaping above
the city. She prayed, "O Fire God, please do not burn Hanuman. And
please, do not allow the innocent to be hurt," and her prayers were heard.

In another long leap, Hanuman landed back on the distant shore
where Jambavan, the monkey soldiers, and Ram himself awaited him.
"Hurry, Lord Ram," he said. "Sita is waiting for you. She gave me her
barrette to bring to you." All the animals said to Ram at once, "Lord, we'll
cross the ocean with you and go to Lanka." But how could they get across?

Ram prayed to the ocean god to find a way to get the animals across the sea to Lanka. "Please help us. My soldiers cannot swim."

"You'll just need some stepping stones," answered the ocean god. "As long as it bears your name and is thrown by Nala, the monkey general, any rock will float."

All the animals scampered around collecting rocks. Hanuman etched Ram's name on each rock and then Nala threw them all into the ocean. Before long, the string of floating rocks extended all the way to the northern shores of Lanka. The army hopped over safely, and set up camp outside the four gates leading to Ravana's kingdom.

Meanwhile, earlier that day, King Ravana had banished Prince Vibhishana from the palace. When Vibishana heard that Ram had landed, he went to join him immediately. Ram saw that the young prince was just and good, and gladly accepted him as an ally. "My evil brother has done enough harm," Vibhishana told Ram. "I will help you defeat him."

Ram gave Ravana many chances to avoid bloodshed. Time and time again, he sent the same message: "Return Sita, and you will be forgiven. Otherwise, you will pay dearly." But Ravana was too arrogant to listen. "Sita is mine, all mine!" he snarled. "Win, no matter what the cost!" he ordered his soldiers.

The demons used all kinds of trickery and dark magic but Ram's army fought valiantly and advanced on the battlefield. However, Ravana's son, Indrajeet, had the power to invoke a deadly weapon called "Brahmastra." He went to his secret grove, lit an invisible smokeless fire, whispered secret mantras to Brahma, and finally poured specially prepared hot oil on the fire from an iron ladle.

A total blackout fell upon the grove. Then out of the intense darkness arose a shimmering white chariot, pulled by four wild horses. Indrajeet mounted the Brahmastra chariot, shook the reins, and dashed to the battlefield.

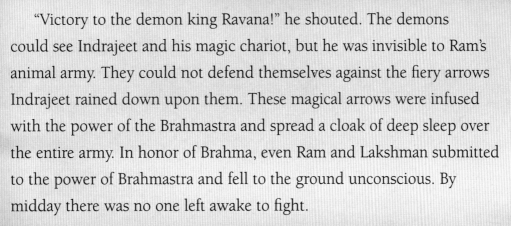

"Victory to the demon king Ravana!" he shouted. The demons could see Indrajeet and his magic chariot, but he was invisible to Ram's animal army. They could not defend themselves against the fiery arrows Indrajeet rained down upon them. These magical arrows were infused with the power of the Brahmastra and spread a cloak of deep sleep over the entire army. In honor of Brahma, even Ram and Lakshman submitted to the power of Brahmastra and fell to the ground unconscious. By midday there was no one left awake to fight.

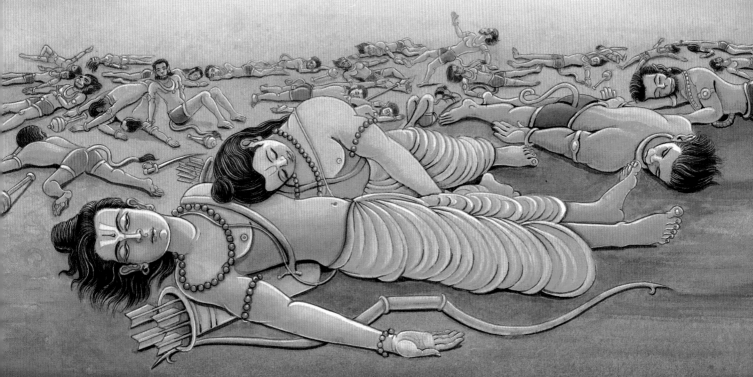

That is, almost no one. The spell of Brahmastra did not hurt Jambavan. He was, after all, Lord Brahma's son. The bear simply pulled the arrow out, rubbed his eyes, and stood up. A few steps away, Prince Vibhishana, who was also unaffected by the spell, was checking on the dead and wounded. Jambavan called to him. "Leave them for now. We first need to find Hanuman. If Hanuman is safe, everyone else will be saved too. Victory will still be within our grasp."

From across the battlefield Hanuman heard these words and sped to Jambavan. "I am fine," he said. "What can I do for you?"

Jambavan, besides being the king of the bears, was a physician as well, and he knew the healing powers of all the herbs and plants. In great haste he tried to teach Hanuman how to identify the herbs he would need, telling him what color flowers and what shape fruits to search for. "These herbs grow on Sanjeevani Mountain, the medicine mountain in the foothills of the Himalayas. Go there at once," he said. "We have no time to spare."

It took Hanuman only a few seconds to travel to the Himalayas. As he landed on the slopes of Sanjeevani Mountain he could see herbs everywhere, glowing in the light of the setting sun, their fruits and flowers sparkling like gemstones. They were beautiful and they looked powerful—but they all looked the same to him. He hesitated over one plant and then another, unsure which to pick. Finally he decided to take them all, and he began to dig at the base of the mountain. "Ah, I see the whole mountain wishes to come with me," he said with a chuckle, and he headed back to Lanka, carrying the entire mountain in the palm of his hand.

Jambavan got to work right away, preparing the concoctions and poultices from the mountain herbs that Hanuman brought to him. Under the old bear's expert care, row upon row of unconscious animal soldiers woke from their deep sleep and rubbed their eyes, their wounds miraculously healed. Cries of "Victory to Hanuman! Victory to Hanuman!" filled the air.

"The whole universe is grateful to you, Hanuman. Thank you for saving our lives!" said Ram.

Now that the animal soldiers were revived, Ram's army advanced once
again on the battlefield and the tide turned quickly in their favor. It was
Lakshman who struck the deciding blow. Using a sacred
weapon given to him by Lord Indra, he released a
razor sharp arrow that killed Ravana's son, Indrajeet.

Ravana roared in anger and sorrow at the loss of his son, but he was far too arrogant and stubborn to surrender. Instead, he chose to duel with Ram. It would be his last battle. After hours of hard combat, Ram aimed a fatal arrow at Ravana's navel and the evil demon's spirit floated away. Finally, the world was freed from Ravana's tyranny. As he had been warned so often, Ravana paid with his life for stealing Sita from Ram.

The noble Prince Vibhishana became the new King of Lanka, and after the coronation he accompanied Ram, Sita, Lakshman, and their army of monkeys on a ride in the flying Pushpaka chariot. In the twinkling of an eye, they reached the kingdom of Ayodhya.

Ram's return to Ayodhya marked the end of a long exile. He had left the kingdom to honor his father's promise: though Ram was the rightful heir, King Dasharatha had decreed that Ram's brother Bharat should rule Ayodhya first. In the fourteen years that Ram spent wandering the earth, he had cleared the world of countless cruel and deceitful demons. He had done well, but oh, how good it felt to come home at last!

In a splendid and elaborate ceremony, Ram was crowned King of Ayodhya. On this happy occasion, everyone received gifts. "I would never have found Sita without your help," Ram said to Hanuman, handing him a long, gleaming necklace. "Will this string of pearls please your heart?"

A while later King Vibhishana spotted Hanuman sitting by himself, popping the pearls into his mouth and crunching them up into little shards. "What are you doing? You shouldn't eat pearls. Spit them out! Don't you know how precious they are?" cried Vibhishana.

"They have no value for me. They do not bear Ram's name," said Hanuman.

"What do you mean? You don't bear Ram's name either—does that mean you too are without value?" teased Vibhishana.

Hanuman looked up. Wordlessly, he split open his own chest with his sharp nails. An image of Ram, Sita, and Lakshman glowed in the center of his heart and the name "Ram" appeared on his body, written over and over again.

Vibhishana fell to his knees in awe. Ram hurried to Hanuman's side, closed the wound with the touch of his fingers, and then embraced the monkey.

"What a truly precious monkey you are! What a wise, courageous, and perfect monkey! Here. Leave these pearls, and take my signet ring instead." Ram slipped his gold signet ring onto Hanuman's finger. "As long as you live on Earth, always be sure to help the meek and innocent."

"Yes my Lord, I will," Hanuman promised and kissed the inscription on the ring—*Ram, Ram, Ram.*

Hanuman has kept his promise to this very day. And he will continue to keep it as long as people recite the Ramayana to remember Ram's story.

⚜

Note to Parents and Teachers

The story of Hanuman, taken from the Valmiki Ramayana, has inspired Indian children and adults alike for thousands of years. It is my hope that this version of the story, retold for American children, will inspire them as well. In India, people revere Hanuman as a positive role model. He is intelligent and clever, powerful and strong, and possesses many magical abilities. With all of these gifts comes responsibility. Hanuman has to make choices: He could side with Vali, the wicked monkey king, or with the good king, Sugriva, whom Vali has deposed. He could side with Ravana, the wicked demon king, or with the virtuous Lord Ram, who has accepted exile to honor a promise made by his father. Hanuman always chooses to side with the good. In his humility and sincere desire to help those who tell the truth, Hanuman uses his gifts wisely. Hanuman's story is meant to encourage children to make good use of their own gifts—to speak up and stand fearlessly against injustice, cruelty, tyranny, and oppression, just as Hanuman stood fearlessly against Ravana's army of ruthless demons.

About the Illustrations

The illustrations were created with watercolor and tempera paints. Using the transparent watercolors, the artist painted each picture in several steps. After outlining the figures, he filled them in, using three tones for each color to achieve a three-dimensional effect; next he applied the background colors. After each step he "fixed" the painting by rinsing it with water until only the paint absorbed by the paper remained.

Then the artist applied a "wash," using the opaque tempera paints. After wetting the painting again, he applied the tempera to the surface until the whole painting appeared to be behind a colored fog. While the wash color was still wet, he used a dry brush to remove it from the faces, hands, and feet of the figures. He let the wash dry completely, then rinsed it again to fix the colors. To achieve the right color and emotional tone, each painting received several washes and fixes. Finally, the artist redefined the delicate line work of each piece, allowing the painting to reemerge from within the clouds of wash.

Please feel free to trace or photocopy this drawing of Hanuman for children to color.